The Christmas Gift

By John McDonnell

Copyright © 2011 John McDonnell

All rights reserved.

ISBN: **1466435585**
ISBN-13: **978-1466435582**

DEDICATION

To my mother, who taught me to believe. To my wife, who showed endless faith in me. To my children, who teach me every day to look for the best in people.

FOREWORD

This little book is becoming more popular each Christmas, and I want to offer my thoughts on why that is.

My father was a boy in Philadelphia during the Great Depression of the 1930s, and I remember vividly the stories he told me about those days. His father never lost his job, but his company cut his hours in half, and the family often did not have enough to eat. Growing up like that left emotional scars on my father that never went away. When he was in his 60s he still could not throw away leftover food -- when you grew up hungry, you learned never to waste food, he told me.

My mother's side of the family was not as poor during the Depression. Her father made enough money for them to live comfortably, but he always gave back to the less fortunate. My mother remembered hungry men who would come to the back door and ask for food, and her mother never turned them down. The Great Depression was a terrible time, but it brought out the best in many people, as they shared what they had with those who had little.

"The Christmas Gift" is a story set in that period, and it's about the power of love and generosity, and how you can change someone's life by a simple act of kindness. In today's hard economic times people are learning those same lessons all over again.

Maybe that's why people like "The Christmas Gift". Simple kindness can be the most life-changing force in the universe.

THE CHRISTMAS GIFT

Constance was the prettiest doll in the collection of Miss Emily Hawthorne, who lived in a big house in Philadelphia that her father built years and years ago. Miss Hawthorne's father was a very wealthy man who owned the biggest department store in the city, and he loved to buy her dolls when she was a little girl.

A long time ago Miss Hawthorne had played with Constance every day. She had dressed her in pretty outfits and had tea parties with her, and curled up next to Constance in bed every night.

Nowadays, though, Constance spent most of her time in a big mahogany display case with the other dolls. Miss Hawthorne had never married or had children of her own, and she was too old to play with dolls, so she put her doll collection in the big case and took them out once a year, when she invited the neighborhood girls in for a tea party at Christmastime.

This Christmas was an especially important time to bring the dolls out, too. It was December of 1937, the start of a particularly bleak winter. There were many people out of work, and groups of men took to traveling around the country looking for anyplace where they could find enough work to pay for a little food, so they could survive another day. Every day people would come to the back door of Miss Hawthorne's mansion and ask for food, and the cook, a big red-faced woman named Annie, had Miss Hawthorne's permission to feed them.

There were rumblings of war in Europe, and people were weighed down by events.

Children know when their parents are worried, and it makes them afraid, because if parents are worried, the world seems unhinged, and the very ground under a child's feet seems to vanish.

This is where a doll comes in handy, because dolls help children take their minds off troubling events in their lives. Most dolls are happy to do this, but Constance had no feeling for it. She thought her job was simply to be pretty, and that people liked her because of her blonde hair, her tiny little red lips, and her beautiful pink satin dresses.

This year Miss Hawthorne had invited a dozen girls to come to her tea party, and they all arrived laughing and bringing that special glow that little girls have. The house seemed brighter, and there was happiness in the air. There were Christmas wreaths everywhere, and gingerbread houses, and the smell of cinnamon and spices, and a ten-foot Blue Spruce tree in the parlor with candy canes and ribbons on it.

Miss Hawthorne and Annie had prepared a lovely afternoon, with teacakes and cookies and little sandwiches and many other good things. All the dolls were primped and prettied, and Constance had her spot at the head of the table, because of course she was the prettiest doll.

The girls were all situated in the dining room, chattering away and laughing gaily, when Annie came in and whispered in Miss Hawthorne's ear.

"There's something you need to see in the kitchen," she said.

Miss Hawthorne went out to the kitchen and found a child sitting at the big wooden table in a threadbare green coat, with a face half-covered by a battered grey hat. The only way you could tell she was a girl was that she carried a faded Raggedy Ann doll.

"I found her in here stealing food," Annie said, with her hands on her hips, and indeed the girl had a half-eaten apple in her hand. "She came in the back door when I was serving the food to the girls in the other room."

The little girl looked like she hadn't eaten in weeks, and Miss Hawthorne peered at her with her brow furrowed.

"What's your name?" she asked.

"Sarah," the girl said. She looked like she couldn't decide if she was angry or ready to cry.

"What's a little girl like you doing stealing food?"

"I was just hungry, is all."

"Where do you live?"

"Nowhere," the girl said. "I travel around. I've been all around the country."

"But where are your parents?"

Sarah didn't answer.

"Answer Miss Hawthorne, or I'll box your ears," Annie said. She spoke sternly, although she didn't look like she'd really box anybody's ears.

"They're gone. My mother's dead, of pneumonia. Father left a few years ago."

"But how do you survive, child?" Miss Hawthorne said. "You can't just traipse around the country by yourself."

"I have some friends. They look out for me."

Annie looked at Miss Hawthorne and shook her head. "What's this country coming to, I'd like to know?" she said.

Miss Hawthorne was silent for a moment. "Well, Sarah," she said. "How would you like to go to a tea party?"

"What?" Annie spluttered. "But, Miss Hawthorne, you can't do that. . . why, she was stealing from us!"

Miss Hawthorne smiled. "Annie, I'm not going to get upset over a little girl who's hungry. We can easily set another place at the table."

Annie grumbled a bit, but eventually she agreed, and went out to find another place setting.

Well, it was a kind gesture, but it was bound to fail. The other girls turned up their noses at this ragamuffin of a girl, and they tried hard to ignore her, although they noticed that Sarah didn't have a clue about how to behave at a tea party. She took more than her share of sandwiches and wolfed them down noisily, wiping her mouth with her sleeve when she was finished.

If the girls were shocked, imagine Constance's horror when Miss Hawthorne gave Sarah the seat next to her, Constance! It was almost too much for a doll to bear, having that dirty little girl put her hands on Constance's beautiful pink dress. Why, she didn't seem to know how to handle a doll, judging from the condition of her Raggedy Ann, who was torn and dirty, and had pieces of her hair missing. The tea party was not turning out the way Constance had expected. She longed for the afternoon to be over, so she could go back in her glass case, away from the grubby hands of this unmannerly young girl.

But it was not to be.

After several hours of torture, Constance felt relief when parents started arriving to pick up their children. The little girls put on their coats and hats and said their goodbyes and thank yous to Miss Hawthorne, and there was much hustle and bustle while Annie gave them brightly wrapped boxes with gifts inside, and bags of cookies to take home.

Nobody seemed to pay attention to Sarah, sitting by herself with Constance, and then, quick as a flash, it happened -- Sarah bolted from the room, ran through the kitchen while Annie's back was turned, and sprang out the back door, carrying Constance.

Constance had never been outside before, and she was so bewildered by all the sights and the noise that she didn't realize at first that Sarah was running through a maze of streets and alleys, not stopping till she was far away from the big house Miss Hawthorne lived in.

Constance wondered where they were going. The sky was getting dark, as it was already 4:00 on a winter afternoon, and there was a brisk wind. Sarah made her way through a network of streets and alleys, and it seemed with each step she was going into a different world than the quiet, tree-lined street that Miss Hawthorne lived on. Here there were houses with broken windows, and trash blowing in the street, and there were knots of men standing around on corners, or huddled around trash cans that had fires burning in them. Their faces were thin and their eyes looked huge, and Constance was frightened of them.

Finally Sarah came to a street that stopped at a fence. Beyond the high wooden fence there came the sound of train whistles and engines steaming by. Sarah found a loose board in the fence and pushed it aside, then climbed through. She went down an embankment and then along a little creek that ran near the train yard. Sarah kept to the bushes by the creek, and wound her way along till she came to a small group of figures huddled around a campfire, a little way up the hill from the stream.

"Is that you, Sarah?" a man's voice said. It sounded rough and raspy, but with a note of kindness in it.

"It's me," Sarah said, drawing closer. "Hello, Bill."

"Where's the food?" Bill said. He had on a cap pulled low over his face, and he was a big man with large hands.

"I didn't get any," Sarah said. "I snuck into the kitchen of a grand big house, but they caught me."

"You were gone for hours," Bill said.

"They fed me," Sarah said. "But I thought they weren't going to let me go. I ran out the back door."

"What's that you have there," Bill said, pointing to Constance. "What is that, a doll? What happened to your Raggedy Ann doll?"

Sarah drew Constance close to her. "The lady at the house gave her to me. Her name is Constance. I traded my Raggedy Ann for her."

"Let me see her," Bill said. Sarah didn't move, but Bill reached over and grabbed Constance out of Sarah's arms. He held Constance up to the flickering light coming from the campfire. "Hm," he said, looking Constance up and down. "Fancy doll. Look at the hair on her." He ran his fingers through Constance's hair.

"This doll won't last a week with us," he said, handing Constance back to Sarah. "She's too delicate. She'll break, or you'll lose her, or she'll get stolen. You should have kept your Raggedy Ann."

"No!" Sarah said. "Nothing's going to happen to her. I'll take good care of her. I promised I'd bring her back. We just traded for awhile."

Constance was furious at all of this. First, Sarah had not traded Raggedy Ann for her, and second, Sarah had never promised anyone that she'd bring Constance back. It was infuriating, how this girl lied!

Bill frowned. "Now, why did you promise something like that? We may not get back here for a long while, honey. You know that. We travel all the time, and we don't know when we'll be back."

Those last words made Constance afraid. Not come back? Ever? Not see Miss Hawthorne ever again? What would become of her? What a state of affairs! It was quite upsetting.

It was sad, too. It was sad because she had lost her home, and her position as the most beautiful of all Miss Hawthorne's dolls.

Later, when the fire was dwindling and the men went to sleep, Sarah took Constance and curled up with her in a makeshift lean-to made out of some old boards and railroad ties, and Constance heard her sobbing softly into her sleeve. The trains in the yard across the way sounded their mournful whistles and then whooshed off into the night, taking people far from their homes. Somehow Constance knew she'd be on one of those trains tomorrow.

And that's exactly what happened. The next day they hopped a freight train bound for Chicago, and Constance got to ride in an empty boxcar with Sarah and Bill. The wind whistled through the slats in the boxcar and it was very noisy as the train rattled over the tracks. Sarah held Constance close, and combed her hair with a little comb she fished out of her pocket. "I will never leave you," she whispered in Constance's ear. "No matter what happens."

And quite a lot did happen.

They had to run to get away from railroad police in Michigan, who were chasing them for hopping trains. They scrambled through some dense woods to get away, and Constance's dress got caught on a thorn bush and ripped.

One day in Albuquerque New Mexico a man tried to steal Constance so he could sell her at a pawnshop. He tried to grab her out of Sarah's arms, but when Sarah resisted and pulled back, the man pulled also, and yanked one of Constance's arms off. Bill tried to reattach the arm but he didn't do a very good job and the arm hung at an odd angle.

In California they found work picking grapes, and Constance spent so much time in the sun by Sarah's side that her skin peeled and got little cracks in it and her dress got faded. Sarah was so tired every night from the farm work that she fell asleep without brushing Constance's hair. In no time Constance's hair was a mess, with tangles and knots, and even little twigs and dirt in it.

Night times were the loneliest. Constance would lie there in Sarah's arms every night and listen to the sounds of the hobo camp. You could hear the low voices of the men talking, and the sound of a harmonica, plus the train whistles with their mournful sound passing through the valley miles away. Constance could hear the sadness in the men's voices as they talked of their families and memories of their homes. Sometimes she would think of her own home, which seemed so far away now, her nice warm house and the rustle of Miss Hawthorne's dresses, the good humor of Annie, the bright lights and the sparkling chandelier in the big dining room. How she missed those tea parties, where she was always the center of attention! Now hardly anyone paid attention to her; they all had so much worrying them that they didn't have room in their lives for a doll.

Except for Sarah. Constance realized that she meant a lot to Sarah. It was such a hard life, and Sarah had so much weighing on her, that Constance didn't know what would happen if she didn't have a doll to take her mind off things. Sarah still cried herself to sleep every night, at least when she wasn't so exhausted that she fell asleep immediately. She hugged Constance close to her, and took her everywhere, never letting her out of her sight.

And then disaster struck. In Butte, Montana, Sarah dropped Constance as she was struggling to jump on a train. Bill had yanked Sarah on the train as it was pulling out of the station, and Sarah dropped Constance next to the tracks beside the train. Sarah screamed and wanted to jump off to get Constance, but Bill held her back. The train pulled away, and Constance lay on the gravel, wondering what was going to happen to her now.

She lay there for a whole day and night, listening to the rumble of the trains as they passed, getting cinders and soot in her hair and dress, and feeling scared.

At night when the stars came out she was especially scared. The world seemed like such a vast, big place and she was such a tiny little doll. What could she do? Why, she couldn't even get up and walk away from this predicament. She was powerless, entirely dependent on someone finding her.

How she longed to be with Sarah again! She felt as if she'd break with grief. She knew now that Sarah needed her so much, and she wanted with all her being to help that little girl. At one point she thought her heart was bursting with sadness. Just then she saw a shooting star arc across the sky, and a sudden calmness came over her. She couldn't say why, but she suddenly felt like everything was going to be all right.

The next morning she heard Sarah's voice off in the distance.

"It was over there," Sarah was saying. "I'm sure I dropped her somewhere over there."

Constance was overjoyed to hear Sarah's voice, but she was terror-stricken that somehow Sarah would not find her. Just then a train whooshed by and drowned out Sarah's voice. The train was very large, with many cars, and it took a long time to go by. Constance was frightened that Sarah would leave before the train finished passing.

If that happened, Constance might be here for a long time. She imagined the years passing slowly, the snow and rain falling on her, the sun baking her in the summer, all the while she was getting more and more dirty from soot and cinders from the passing trains. Maybe someday a maintenance man would find her, a dirty, broken doll by the side of the tracks, and he'd just toss her in the nearest trash bin, and she'd be ground up with all the other trash, or burned in an incinerator, or just buried somewhere in the earth.

It was such an appalling prospect that Constance felt devastated and very, very sad. The worst part about it, she thought, was that she would be gone forever from Sarah's life. She couldn't bear to think of that poor girl without a doll to comfort her. Constance wanted so badly to comfort Sarah, to be a part of her life, that she almost felt like she could cry. And then an amazing thing happened -- she felt a teardrop forming under her eye. But of course that couldn't be so -- it was probably condensation, like the dew that formed on the flowers every morning.

Then the train passed with a final whoosh, and Constance heard Sarah's voice coming down the track.

"She has to be here somewhere," Sarah said. "It was right along here that I dropped her. Oh, look! Is that her, on the side of the track?"

Then there was the sound of footsteps running along the gravel, and in moments Sarah was there, and she picked Constance up and hugged her close, crying with joy.

"I found her, I found her!" she was shouting and crying at the same time, and Constance could feel Sarah's heart beating wildly as the little girl held her close to her chest. It was the most warm and wonderful feeling, like being enveloped in a big bubble of love.

"My beautiful, wonderful Constance," Sarah said, kissing her all over. "I'm so glad I found you. I won't ever let anything bad happen to you again, I promise."

And I won't leave you, Constance thought. Somehow, I will find a way to stay with you. It was strange, this feeling inside. It was something Constance had never felt before -- tenderness toward a child.

That night Sarah and Bill hopped another train, this time headed east. Sarah held Constance to her chest while she looked out the boxcar at the world passing by, and she said: "Don't worry, Constance. I'm taking you back to Miss Hawthorne. Bill was right, this wasn't a good life for a doll like you. Why, look at you -- you're a wreck. Your hair is tangled, your arm is broken, and your dress is torn. I should never have brought you with me. It was selfish of me, and I'm sorry. But don't worry; we'll be back in Philadelphia by tomorrow, and then you'll be back in your nice big home again."

Constance wished she could talk so much, she almost felt that she would burst. She wanted to tell Sarah that it wasn't her fault, that she didn't care about how she looked as long as she made Sarah happy. She didn't want to go back to Miss Hawthorne now. That had been a nice life, but somehow this seemed to be her place; with Sarah. She wanted to stay with this girl through all the ups and downs of her life, no matter what happened or how she looked. She just wanted to be there so there wouldn't be such a big hole in Sarah's life.

Sarah fell asleep with Constance next to her, and Constance could feel Sarah's heart beating, and also a wheezing in Sarah's chest. Sarah had a cough these days that never went away, and she seemed tired all the time. She had dark circles under her eyes, and Constance worried there was something wrong with her.

Sometimes, Constance realized, there was great sadness in being a doll. For dolls can't put their arms around a little girl, or sing a lullaby to her, or do anything for her. They just have to be. And that's what Constance was learning, that she had to simply be, and let the magic work.

The next day, just as the sun was coming up, Sarah and Bill jumped off the train at the train yard in Philadelphia. They snuck through the yard so as not to be seen, then climbed over a fence and headed for a familiar spot where other hobos gathered under a bridge in a wooded area of Fairmount Park. It was early still, and Sarah shivered in the cold as they walked. There was a fire going and a group of men huddled around it when they reached the bridge.

Sarah and Bill joined the group and warmed themselves by the fire. Constance listened as the men talked about mutual friends and adventures they'd had on the road, and if they'd found any work. They all looked so downtrodden and sad, and Constance realized this life was aging them. She noticed lines in their faces that hadn't been there when she'd last seen some of them.

"How's prospects, boys?" Bill said. "Any work out here?"

"Things are getting worse," one of the men, a grizzled fellow with a gray stubble of beard, said. "Not much work of any kind anymore."

The rest of the men nodded. "You can't find nothing," another man said. "I gave up looking. I just go to the soup kitchen every day to get my meal, 'cause there ain't no work anywhere."

Constance could see there was fear in Bill's eyes. "Nothing? I can do a little carpentry. Nothing available for a man who can work with his hands?"

The men shook their heads. "There's no jobs," one man said. "No building going on. Nobody's got the money."

Bill's big frame shivered, and he put his hands out to feel the heat from the fire. The weather was getting colder, and there were even a few snowflakes falling, dusting the ground with a thin cover of white. It was late December, a year since Sarah had taken Constance away from Miss Hawthorne's house.

One of the men had a bag of day-old rolls he'd gotten from a bakery as payment for sweeping the floor, and he gave them out to the group. Sarah and Bill ate the rolls hungrily, as if they were the most delicious breakfast in the world.

Then they broke off from the group and went to talk by themselves.

"We can't stay here," Bill said. "There's no work, and winter is coming. We have no place to stay, no food. You've had a cough for weeks,

Sarah, and this cold weather ain't going to help that. We're going to have to leave. We'll head down south. Maybe there will be work there."

Sarah looked sad, but she shook her head in agreement. "Okay," she said. "But we can't leave till I take Constance back to Miss Hawthorne. I can't take care of her, living like this. I have to take her back."

"All right, honey," Bill said. "But you have to do it today. We need to get out of here."

The rest of the day Sarah seemed to clutch Constance to her even closer, in preparation for giving her away. She held Constance to her chest as she went about asking for food from people on the city streets, knocking on doors in wealthy neighborhoods and asking for scraps.

Constance did not want to leave her. She felt like she could burst from sadness at the thought of leaving this little girl with the dirty face. Isn't there something I could do for her? she thought. She wanted so much to help her.

Late in the afternoon, Sarah finally got back to Miss Hawthorne's neighborhood, and then found her way to the big house at the end of the driveway. The snow had been falling down lazily all day, but now it was coming down faster, and Sarah hunched over in her thin coat, coughing and wheezing in the face of the driving snow. She made her way to the back door, and knocked.

The door opened, and there was the cook. She didn't seem to recognize Sarah at first, but then her eyes widened when she saw Constance.

"Why, are you the little girl that stole Miss Hawthorne's doll?" she said.

"Yes," Sarah said. "Is Miss Hawthorne home? I'd like to give Constance back to her.

Annie whistled. "Give her back? In that condition? She looks a wreck. Miss Hawthorne won't be happy with that."

"I know she doesn't look very good," Sarah said. "I didn't do a good job of taking care of her, I'm afraid. I just want to give her back, and then I'll be gone."

Annie opened the door wide, and said, "Come in, then. I'll go get Miss Hawthorne."

Inside, the kitchen was bright and warm, and delicious smells filled the air. Sarah sat down at the big oak table and waited. She held Constance tightly to her, and whispered. "Well, this is goodbye, Constance. I'm so glad I had the chance to be with you this last year. I'm sorry I didn't take care of you the way I should have. I hope you'll forgive me."

Constance wanted so much to tell her not to feel that way. Why can't I talk? she thought. Why can I feel all these feelings but not be able to express them? Why was I made a doll? What kind of a life is that?

Then the door opened and Miss Hawthorne came into the kitchen. She looked at Constance first, and her eyes grew wide. Was she shocked at how Constance looked? Was she horrified? Disappointed? Sad? Constance couldn't tell, but then Miss Hawthorne looked at Sarah, and her face melted. She rushed over and put her arms around Sarah, and hugged her tight.

"Oh, Sarah," she said. "You look like you've been through a lot. Are you all right? You look, well" -- she paused -- "so much thinner."

"I'm okay," Sarah said, brushing a hair out of her face.

"I bet you could use a good meal," Miss Hawthorne said. "You look like you haven't eaten in days."

"No," Sarah said. "Not very much."

"Annie," Miss Hawthorne said. "I have an idea. Could you make us a nice lunch to have in the dining room? I think Sarah and I could use that."

"Coming right up," Annie said.

They went into the dining room, and it was decorated for Christmas, but Sarah barely seemed to notice. She was wheezing softly as she walked, and Constance didn't like the sound of that.

She found a chair to sit in, and slumped listlessly in it. She didn't even perk up when Miss Hawthorne brought her Raggedy Ann in, all fixed up good as new.

Miss Hawthorne tried to cheer her up. "Look," she said. "Here's your Raggedy Ann doll. Doesn't she look pretty?" She sat the Raggedy Ann doll on Constance's lap, but Constance barely seemed to notice her.

What's the matter with her? Raggedy Ann said, in the special, silent way that dolls talk. *She looks terrible. I've never seen her look that bad.*

It was a bad year, Constance said. *A lot of bad things happened. There wasn't enough to eat. Sarah and Bill suffered a lot.*

Well, you don't look so good yourself, Raggedy Ann said.

Yes, I'm the worse for wear. It ages you to live outside.

I know, Raggedy Ann said.

How do you like living here? Constance said.

It's simply grand. Although the other dolls don't like me. They think I'm beneath them.

Oh, I can believe that, Constance said. *I was like that too. But I've seen the wider world now, and been through some hard times, and I don't feel that way anymore. How is Miss Hawthorne?* she asked.

She has been worrying about you and Sarah a lot in this past year, Raggedy Ann said.

She looks older. There are lines in her face.

She is sad a lot, and lonely. It is lonely for her living in this big house.

She was never lonely before. She had me, and the other dolls.

It was not enough. This is like living in a museum, Constance. A human needs to feel love. Her heart was almost closed, you know, until she met Sarah. Sarah has made her feel love again.

Constance looked at Miss Hawthorne and noticed for the first time how old she looked. She had worry lines around her eyes, and her hair seemed whiter than before. Miss Hawthorne was looking at Sarah with such pain in her eyes.

Just then Sarah started coughing again, and this time her coughing fit went on for longer than usual. Miss Hawthorne wrung her hands with worry while Sarah's face turned red and she doubled over from the coughing.

Then something shocking happened. Sarah coughed up blood, a bit of blood, on the white rug. Miss Hawthorne's eyes widened, and she said, "My goodness, child, you're very sick."

"It's nothing," Sarah said. "I do that sometimes."

"It's not 'nothing'," Miss Hawthorne said. "You are a very sick child." She came over and felt Sarah's head. "And you have a fever. You need to get to bed right now."

Sarah started shivering, but she protested. "No, I have to go. My friend Bill will be worried."

"I insist," Miss Hawthorne said. "You can't go out in that snowstorm in your condition. Come, we'll get you in bed and call the doctor."

Miss Hawthorne bundled Sarah up in a big four-poster bed in the upstairs bedroom where she kept all the dolls, and then left to call the doctor. She came back later with some soup and toast, but Sarah was too feverish to touch it. Later, the doctor came. He was a kindly man with wire-rimmed glasses and a shock of unruly gray hair, and he examined Sarah with care. He looked at her with narrowed eyes and worry in his face. He peered down her throat, made her say "Ah," looked in her ears, listened to her chest, all the while Miss Hawthorne was looking on, wringing her hands with worry.

Finally the doctor said, "You are very sick, young lady. I recommend that you drink fluids, have Miss Hawthorne put cold compresses on you, and get some rest. I will come back in the morning to check on you."

Outside in the hallway, he closed the bedroom door and said, "It is very worrisome. She is very sick, Miss Hawthorne. There is not much I can do for her. If she develops pneumonia it will be very bad. You must pray for her."

Miss Hawthorne did her duty; faithfully putting cold compresses on Sarah's head throughout the night, and trying to get her to drink some juice, for her fever was very high.

And then something amazing happened. When Miss Hawthorne had left for a while, the door opened and a man came in wearing a red suit and a funny red stocking cap. He was very short but stout, and had white hair and a full white beard. He strode over to the bed and looked down at Sarah with kind eyes.

Sarah was sleeping soundly, and she was not aware of him. Then he turned to Constance and said, "Do you know who I am?"

"Are you Miss Hawthorne's father?" Sarah said. She was surprised to hear herself talk. The man seemed to think that was very funny, and he shook with laughter. His laugh was a wondrous thing, like music, or the feeling of sitting in front of a warm fire, and it seemed to make the room grow brighter. "No, my dear," he said, finally, "I am not Miss Hawthorne's father."

"Then who are you?"

"Just a man who believes in the power of toys," he said. He looked at Sarah again. "You love her very much, don't you?"

"Yes," Constance said. She was surprised to hear herself talking.

"Talk to her then," the man said. "She needs to hear that from you. After all, you are a doll, and you can help a child like this."

"Are you sure?" Constance said. She didn't know if it was right for a doll to talk to a little girl.

"It's perfectly okay," the man said, laughing. "Now go ahead, my child, talk to her."

Constance turned to Sarah and said, "Sarah, you are loved very much. You are not alone. Please get better, get all better, so that you may have a long life. You are destined to have a long and full life, with many children, but you must get better tonight."

Constance didn't know where those words came from, and she turned to see if the man had heard them, but to her surprise he was gone.

And then a shocking thing happened. Constance saw Sarah's spirit start to leave her body. It was like a wisp of starlight that came out of her head, and started to drift toward the ceiling.

"No," Constance said. "No, Sarah, please don't go. You are needed here. Miss Hawthorne needs you. She is a lonely old woman, and she needs the sparkle of a child in her life. Raggedy Ann told me how desperately lonely she is. If you go, her heart will get smaller and smaller, till there's nothing left of it. Only you can save her, Sarah. Please, stay."

The starlight pooled at the ceiling, and then, slowly, it came back down and entered Sarah's forehead.

Sarah slept more peacefully after that, and Constance could feel her temperature going down. The next morning when Miss Hawthorne came in Sarah was sitting up in bed, and Miss Hawthorne was so happy she looked like she was going to cry. When the doctor came back, he examined Sarah and said, "I don't know what happened, but this young lady is in much better shape than when I left here last night. I think she's going to be all right."

Miss Hawthorne clapped her hands and said, "Oh, I think that is the best Christmas gift I ever got!"

When she said that, Constance realized that it was Christmas morning, and that the man she'd seen last night was Santa Claus. It had been many years since she'd seen him, and she'd almost forgotten who he was.

Annie made a big breakfast of eggs and ham and toast, and a pitcher of fresh-squeezed orange juice and a steaming mug of hot cocoa, and Sarah ate it all with great spirit, finishing every crumb.

Miss Hawthorne was so happy she was sitting on the bed chattering away, just full of plans.

"Sarah," she said. "I did a lot of thinking last night, and I have an idea. I want you to move in with me. I'll get my lawyers to do the paperwork so that I can adopt you. There's no need for you to go back to living the way you did before. Why, it almost killed you. You can live here with me and Annie, and we'll have a wonderful life."

"But what about Bill?" Sarah said. "He's been so nice to me, almost like a father."

"I thought of that," Miss Hawthorne said. "I've already spoken to the man who runs my father's department store, and he said they could hire Bill to work in the stockroom, or drive a truck, or any one of a dozen other jobs. I've never asked him for a favor, and he'll certainly do this for me."

"You would do that?" Sarah said. "That's very kind of you, and it will make Bill happy. He just wants a job; that's all he ever wanted. He doesn't like taking charity from people."

"I'm happy to help," Miss Hawthorne said. "Now, what about you, Sarah? Will you take me up on my offer? How about moving in with me and Annie?"

Sarah considered it for a moment.

Please say yes, Constance thought. Please, please say yes.

"I guess I could try it out," Sarah said. "Maybe stay for a little while."

"Oh, that would be grand," Miss Hawthorne said. "Just grand!"

Then Sarah seemed to notice Constance for the first time since last night. "Oh, I'm so ashamed of what's happened to Constance. I really ruined her. I'm sorry for stealing her," she said. She held the doll out to Miss Hawthorne and said, "Here. I hope you can fix her, so she'll look nice in the display case again."

"Oh, no," Miss Hawthorne said. "She's not going back in the display case, not ever again. We'll get her fixed up, but I want her to be your doll, from now on, and you can take her anywhere you want."

"Really?" Sarah said. "You mean that?"

"I certainly do," Miss Hawthorne said. "Dolls are not meant to be put on a shelf and taken out once a year. They're made for companionship. They need to be by a little girl's side, right there through all the good and bad times. They play an important role, and it's been that way for, oh, thousands of years."

Sarah hugged Constance to her tightly, and said, "Thank you so much. I'll take good care of her, I promise. I'll keep her with me always, and I'll share all my secrets with her."

Constance could hear Sarah's heart beating, and she was happy.

She was happy to be part of the life of a little girl. She realized, of course, that Sarah would eventually grow older and have less time for her, but somehow she knew that Sarah would have little girls of her own, and that she would be part of their lives, and then they would have children. . . and she would keep playing a role in some little girl's life for many years to come.

It was a wonderful feeling, and it felt like. . . home.

THE END

ABOUT THE AUTHOR

John McDonnell has been a writer for many years and has written on many topics, but "The Christmas Gift" is nearest to his heart. John lives outside of Philadelphia with his wife and four children. For more of John's books, visit his author page at Amazon: http://www.amazon.com/-/e/B004AXGYHQ, or his author page at Smashwords: http://www.smashwords.com/profile/view/jaymack

Printed in Great Britain
by Amazon